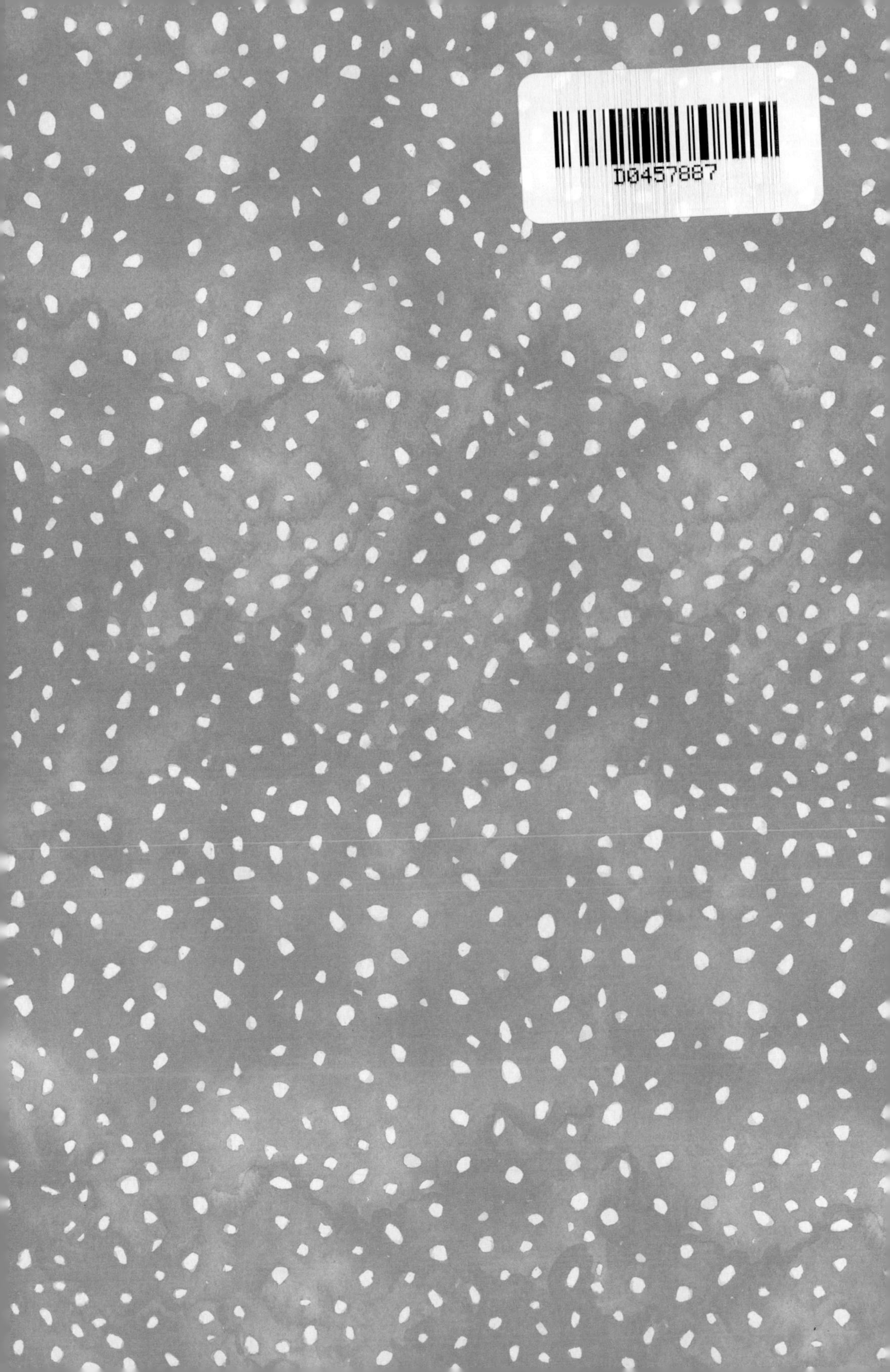
D0457887

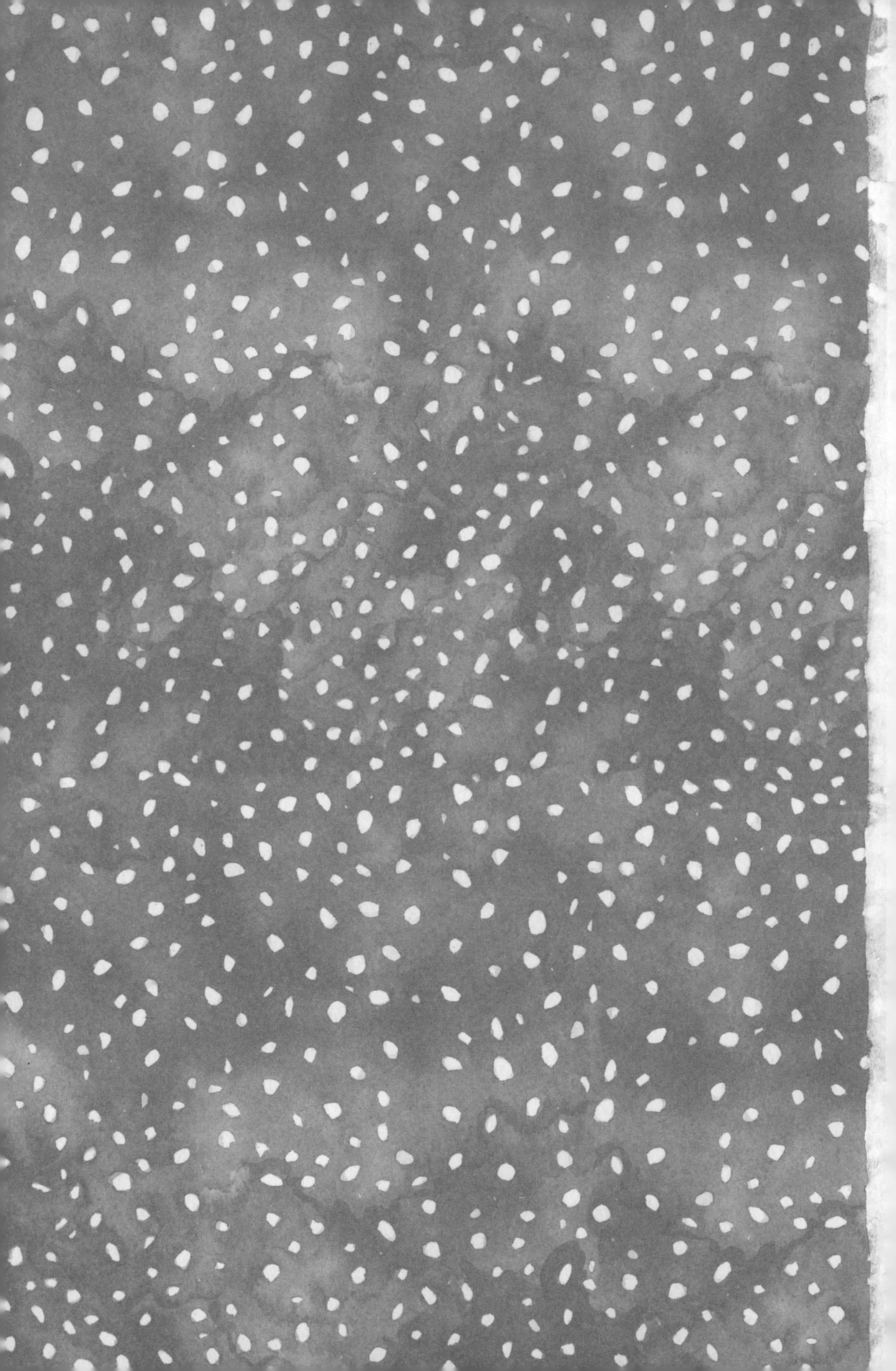

ANNIE and SIMON

Banana Muffins and Other Stories

Catharine O'Neill

Candlewick Press

First edition 2017

Library of Congress Catalog Card Number 2015941710
ISBN 978-0-7636-7498-4

17 18 19 20 21 22 TLF 10 9 8 7 6 5 4 3 2 1

Printed in Dongguan, Guangdong, China

This book was typeset in Berkeley
with hand lettering by the author-illustrator.
The illustrations were done in watercolor.

Candlewick Press
99 Dover Street
Somerville, Massachusetts 02144

visit us at www.candlewick.com

Contents

CHAPTER ONE

Banana Muffins

Annie and Hazel the dog wandered into the kitchen. Annie's big, big brother, Simon, sat on the floor, polishing his boots.

"Simon, can you make my lunch? Mummy and Daddy are still at the store."

"It's only ten thirty," said Simon.

"But I'm hungry," said Annie.

"I guess I'm a little hungry, too," said Simon. He got up and took two splotchy bananas out of a bowl.

"They look yucky," said Annie.

"But these bananas are just right for making muffins," said Simon.

"Oh, goody," said Annie.

Simon pulled out a cookbook. "Here's something . . . *Banana Muffins with Walnuts and Cranberries.*"

"What about chocolate chips?" asked Annie.

"Nope," said Simon, "it doesn't say anything about chocolate chips."

"Are you sure?" asked Annie.

"I'm sure," said Simon.

Annie helped Simon get out all the stuff they needed.

"I'll measure. You mix," said Simon.

"I'll count, too," said Annie.

Simon poured a cup of sugar into the bowl.

"One," said Annie.

Simon cut a stick of butter into pieces.

"Lots of ones," said Annie. She tried to mix the butter and sugar together with a big wooden spoon. "This is hard."

"I can help," said Simon.

Annie gave Hazel the spoon to lick.

"Ahem." Simon washed the spoon.

"Now two eggs," said Simon.

"I can break the eggs," said Annie. "I learned how at nursery school."

Annie cracked an egg on the side of the bowl and dropped it in. "One." Annie cracked another egg. "Two." Annie looked in the bowl. "Whoopsie, Simon! Eggshells fell in."

"Not to worry," said Simon. He fished the eggshell bits out of the bowl.

"Next flour, baking powder, and salt," said Simon, "all sifted together."

Annie turned the handle of the sifter. "This is hard, too. Go away, Hazel."

"I can help," said Simon.

Together Annie and Simon sifted a white cloud into the bowl.

“Very nice,” said Simon. “OK, nuts and berries, one-half cup each.”

“I’ll count the nuts,” said Annie. “One . . . two . . . three . . .”

“Good grief,” said Simon.

“Thirteen . . . fourteen . . . fifteen . . .”

Annie dropped the nuts into the batter and gave it a stir.

"Now the berries," said Annie. "One . . . two . . . three . . ."

"I think I'll take a nap," said Simon. He put his head down on the kitchen table.

"Twenty . . . twenty-one . . . twenty-two . . ."

Annie got a package out of the cupboard. "One . . . two . . ."

"What are you doing now?" asked Simon.

"Nothing," said Annie.

Simon sat up. "Chocolate chips? Ohhh, no."

"Maybe you changed your mind," said Annie.

"I did not," said Simon. "And this is taking forever. I'm going to finish the muffins by myself." Simon took the bowl from Annie.

"No fair!" said Annie.

Simon measured the milk and mashed the bananas. He stirred them into the batter.

Annie glared at Simon's back.

While Simon greased the tin, Annie shook a bunch of chocolate chips into the batter and gave it a stir.

Then she crawled under the table. Hazel crawled under, too.

"Holy smoke!" said Simon, frowning at the batter. He bent over to look at Annie under the table.

"You weren't nice!" said Annie.

"I wasn't trying to be nice," said Simon. "Little sisters, aarrrrgh! Move over, Hazel."

Simon crawled under the table, too. He patted Hazel. Nobody said anything.

"I could take all the chocolate chips out," said Annie after a while.

Simon sighed. "Maybe the muffins won't taste so bad," he said. "Let's go spoon the batter into the tin."

"OK, Simon."

Annie helped Simon put the batter into the tin and the tin into the oven.

Soon everyone smelled the baking muffins.

"Mmmm, they smell nice," said Annie.

"Like chocolate," said Simon. He took the hot tin out of the oven and the hot muffins out of the tin. When the muffins were cool enough, Annie and Simon each had a taste.

“Oooooh,” said Annie.

“Hey,” said Simon, “I kind of like the chocolate chips.”

“Oh, boy!” said Annie.

Simon had another bite. He thought for a moment. “Maybe I was a little cranky,” he said.

"Oh, you were a lot cranky," said Annie.

Simon frowned.

"I was cranky, too," said Annie.

"There you go," said Simon. "By the way, how many chocolate chips did you put in?"

"I didn't count," said Annie.

"Well," said Simon, "it was exactly the right number."

Annie leaned on Simon's knee. "You know, Simon, I think I mostly like you."

"I think I mostly like you, too, Annie."

CHAPTER TWO

The Baby

One breezy morning, Simon hung up his wet laundry. Annie played with her doll. Hazel carried her toys behind the tree, and then she brought them back again.

"Theo from next door is coming to our house!" sang Annie. "A little baby! I can't wait!"

"Yup," said Simon. "Now I've got to babysit both of you."

"You don't have to babysit me, Simon. I live here."

"That's true. You do," said Simon.

"And I'm not a baby," said Annie. "Here they come!"

Annie hid behind the tree.

Annie listened to Simon and Theo's dad talking over the fence. "Here's Theo, Simon, and his blanket and his moose."

Theo's dad gave his baby a kiss. "Be good, little baby, and hang on to Mr. Moose." Theo's dad lifted Theo gently across the fence and into Simon's arms. "I'll be back in an hour, Simon." And off he went.

"Hello, baby," said Simon, sitting down on the grass with Theo and his purple moose. Annie came out from behind the tree.

"Wow," said Annie. "A baby."

"Yup," said Simon.

Annie sat and gazed at Theo. Theo grabbed Annie's hand. He smiled a sweet smile.

"I'll finish hanging my laundry," said Simon. He held up the last two wet socks. "One green sock and one stripy red sock," he said. "I seem to be missing something. . . ."

Annie wasn't listening. "Simon, can I hold Theo?"

"If you sit in the big chair you can."

So Annie climbed into the big chair, and Simon put Theo on her lap.

"Put this arm here and that arm there," said Simon.

"Don't go away," said Annie.

“I’ll be right here,” said Simon.

Hazel came to see what was going on. She sniffed at Theo and gave him a kiss.

“No, no!” said Annie.

Theo held up his arms and laughed. He pulled Hazel’s ear. Hazel went away.

“What a happy baby,” said Annie.

But Theo didn’t stay happy for long. He stopped laughing. He looked around. Then he beat his hands in the air. “Waah!” he cried.

“What’s the matter, Theo?” asked Simon.

“Where’s his purple moose? I think Theo dropped it,” said Annie.

"Not to worry," said Simon. He looked behind, under, and all around the chair.

"That's odd," said Simon. "I don't see it."

Theo cried, "Waaah!"

"Simon," said Annie, "keep looking!"

"But where could it be?" said Simon. "Annie, try giving Theo your dolly. Just for now."

“OK, Simon.”

But Theo wanted his own purple moose.

“WAAAAH!” yelled Theo.

“Yikes,” said Simon.

Hazel came to see what was going on. Then she went away again.

“Simon, jump around and do your silly dance. That will make Theo stop crying.”

“Oh, for heaven’s sake,” said Simon, but he went ahead and did his silly dance.

Theo watched. He cried a little bit less. "WAAH." And a little bit less. "Waah."

“It’s kind of working,” said Annie. “Now do your upside-down trick, Simon.”

“That’s my best one,” said Simon, “but it takes a bit of getting ready.” Simon put his hands on the ground and his head in his hands. Slowly he raised one leg and then the other, straight up in the air.

"Oh, that's good!" said Annie. "Look, Theo."

Theo watched Simon. "Unh," he said.

Hazel came to see what was going on.

"Hazel," said Simon, "don't flap that thing in my face! I can't see." Simon wobbled over.

“Simon,” said Annie, “look what Hazel has!”

“A stripy red sock,” said Simon. “Fancy that.”

Annie and Simon looked at Hazel.

“You know,” said Annie, “Hazel’s dug a new hole behind the tree. I saw it.”

Simon picked up Theo. “Let’s go see,” he said.

Everyone crouched around Hazel's hole.

"Lord love a duck!" said Simon.

"Hazel took my doll," said Annie.

"And my green sock and my stripy red sock," said Simon.

"And Theo's purple moose," said Annie.

Annie gave Theo his purple moose. Annie gave Simon his two socks. She dusted off her dolly.

"Hazel, you are a naughty dog," she said. Hazel wagged her tail. Annie gave Hazel a kiss.

Annie hung Simon's socks on the side of the laundry basket. Then she sat down next to Simon and Theo.

"Thank you, Annie," said Simon. "And look—I think Theo's about to fall asleep."

Theo blinked slowly.

"No more crying baby," said Simon.

"He's a little sleepyhead," said Annie.

Annie spread Theo's blanket on the grass. Simon laid Theo down on the blanket.

"Babysitting is so great," said Annie. She patted Theo's little arm.

"It wasn't bad," said Simon. "It could have been worse."

"Now comes the best part, Simon."

"Yup," said Simon. "Now we get to watch the socks dry."

"That's not it," said Annie. "Now we get to watch a baby sleep!"

Simon tapped his chin and wiggled his toes. "Hey," he said, "why didn't I think of that?"

CHAPTER THREE

The Bobo

Annie found Simon with his book on Pinecone Rock. Annie sat down on top of him.

"Oof!" said Simon.

"I packed some of my precious stuff to bring to Pickerel Lake, Simon. Want to see?"

"Do I have to open my eyes?" asked Simon.

"No," said Annie. She took something wooden out of her bag and gave it a whirl.

"Not that peacock rattle!" said Simon.

Simon uncovered his ears and opened his eyes. "What else have you got?"

Annie popped something small and round into her mouth.

"Huh," said Simon. "You used to call that a bobo."

Annie took the pacifier out of her mouth. "I found it in my treasure chest, Simon."

“Well, you never did use it,” said Simon, “and now you’re too old.”

“I like it,” said Annie. And she popped the bobo back into her mouth.

“Next,” said Simon.

Annie held a book over Simon’s head.

"A Child's Guide to Butterflies," read Simon. "Hey, I remember this book. It used to be mine."

Simon took the book from Annie and opened it up. "Hey, look at this! Look at that! I forgot about this! Wow!"

Annie made a happy face. She looked at the butterfly book with Simon.

“Woof! Woof! Woof!” Hazel tried to play with Annie’s bobo.

“Leth go loog for budderflieth,” said Annie.

“That thing looks silly, Annie. You can’t even talk.”

“I gan doo dawg.”

"Well," said Simon, "let's walk up to the meadow where the flowers are. Butterflies like flowers."

"Mmmh!" said Annie.

Annie and Simon and Hazel wandered through the meadow, up and down, around and around. There were lots of flowers—yellow, pink, white, and blue.

"Where'th the budderflieth, Thimon?"

"I don't know. . . ." Simon scratched his head. "Maybe it's too cool and cloudy for butterflies. Let's come back when the sun's out."

"Whad'll we do now, Thimon?"

"Woof, woof! Woof, woof, woof!" Hazel barked and barked and barked some more.

"We could find out why Hazel's making such a racket," said Simon.

"Maybe Hathel'th found thomething, Thimon. I'll go thee."

Annie clambered through the flowers and climbed up over the rock.

Hazel HAD found something. . . .

“A borgybine!” cried Annie.

“Thi-i-i-mon!”

Annie took the bobo out of her mouth.

“S-I-I-I-I-I-MON!”

"Here I am," said Simon. He leaped up onto the rock. "Holy smoke, a porcupine!"

"That's what I said," said Annie.

"Hazel," said Simon, "come HERE! Come here RIGHT NOW!"

But Hazel wouldn't come. And she wouldn't stop barking.

She danced around and around the porcupine.

The porcupine stamped its feet and twitched its tail.

"Is it going to bite Hazel?" asked Annie.

"No," said Simon, "but one whack of that tail and Hazel will be a pincushion."

"Oh, Simon, go get her!"

"Then I'll be a pincushion, too!" said Simon.

"I know what! I know what!" Annie popped the bobo back into her mouth and took the rattle out of her pocket. She gave it a whirl.

Hazel turned her head. The porcupine turned its head.

But neither moved.

"What about this?" said Simon. He plucked the bobo out of Annie's mouth.

"Hey!" said Annie.

"Fetch, Hazel!" said Simon. He pretended to toss the bobo into the meadow.

Hazel bounded off.

"Look, Simon! It's working. The porcupine's going away."

The porcupine ambled over to a tree, climbed slowly up the trunk, and curled up on a long branch.

"Well," said Simon, "that is something!"

"Imagine having all those prickles," said Annie. "It would be hard to play. How long is he going to stay up there, Simon?"

“Probably as long as we stay down here,” said Simon.

Hazel trotted back from the meadow. “Good dog,” said Annie.

“Lucky dog,” said Simon.

Everyone looked at the porcupine. The porcupine looked at everyone.

“I like his face, Simon.”

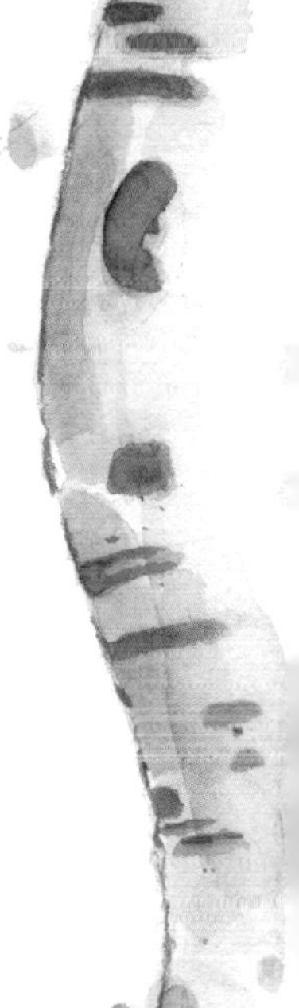

Annie and Simon climbed down off the big rock. Annie held out her hand. “A raindrop, Simon. I hope my precious stuff doesn’t get wet.”

“That stuff got us into and out of a pickle with a porcupine,” said Simon.

"That's why it's precious, Simon. Still, I might let you keep the bobo."

"Gosh," said Simon.

"I'm too old for it," said Annie.

"Well then," said Simon, "I guess you're a little old for a rattle, too. I could keep the bobo *and* the rattle."

"No-o-o-o, Simon."

"I didn't think so," said Simon with a sigh. He gazed up at the sky. "Look, Annie! The clouds are blowing away. The sun is coming out. . . ."

"Let's go find the butterflies," said Annie.